My "p" Sound Box®

WRITTEN BY JANE BELK MONCURE • ILLUSTRATED BY REBECCA THORNBURGH

The Child's World®
childsworld.com

Published by The Child's World®
1980 Lookout Drive • Mankato, MN 56003-1705
800-599-READ • www.childsworld.com

ISBN HARDCOVER: 9781503823198
ISBN PAPERBACK: 9781503831414
LCCN: 2017960372

Printed in the United States of America
PA02371

A NOTE TO PARENTS AND EDUCATORS:

Magic moon machines and five fat frogs are just a few of the fun things you can share with children by reading books with them. Reading aloud helps children in so many ways! It introduces them to new words, motivates them to develop their own reading skills, and expands their attention span and listening abilities. So it's important to find time each day to share a book or two . . . or three!

As you read with young children, you can help develop their understanding of how print works by talking about the parts of the book—the cover, the title, the illustrations, and the words that tell the story. As you read, use your finger to point to each word, modeling a gentle sweep from left to right.

Simple word games help develop important prereading skills, including an understanding of rhyme and alliteration (when words share the same beginning sound, such as "six" and "sand"). Try playing with words from a book you've just shared: "What other words start with the same sound as moon?" "Cat and hat, do those words rhyme?" The possibilities are endless—and so are the rewards!

My "p" Sound Box®

Little  had a box. "I will find things

that begin with my **p** sound," she said.

"I will put them into my sound box."

Little  found a poodle and her puppy.

Did she put the poodle and the puppy into the box? She did.

Then Little  found a pig and piglets in a pigpen.

Did she put the pig and piglets into the box

with the poodle and the puppy? She did.

Little  walked down a path to the park.

In the park, she saw a peach tree. She put some peaches into her box.

Under the peach tree, Little  saw

a picnic table and a picnic basket.

"Let's have a picnic," said Little . She opened the picnic basket and found peanuts, pickles, popcorn, and pie.

Little  and the animals ate until

the pig said, "I am about to pop!"

Little  put the animals back into the box.

She also put back the leftover peanuts, pickles, popcorn, and pie. Now the box was so full, it was about to pop!

Then Little  saw a pony pulling

a cart. "Please pull us!" she said.

The pony pulled them down the
path. They saw a porcupine.

Little gave the porcupine some popcorn. She

put him into the box . . . carefully. He was prickly!

The pony pulled them down the
path. Soon they saw a peacock.

Little  gave the peacock some peanuts.

Then she put him into the box.

Suddenly, the pony stopped.

A panther was in the path!

The pony pranced! The pig, piglets, poodle, puppy, peacock, and porcupine fell out of the box.

The panther pounced on the box.

He ate up all the peanuts, pickles, peaches, popcorn, and pie. Then he smiled politely.

Just then, a  police officer came down the path. "You have found our pet panther," he said. "We will take him back to the zoo."

"Let's take all of my pets to the petting zoo," said Little .

They had a parade . . .

all the way to the petting zoo.

Little 's Word List

panther

parade

park

path

peach

peacock

peanut

pickle

picnic

picnic basket

picnic table

pie

pig

piglet

pigpen

police officer

pony

poodle

popcorn

porcupine

puppy

28

Other Words with Little

pan

pancake

panda

pants

parachute

parrot

pelican

pencil

penguin

penny

piano

pin

pineapple

pizza

plane

plate

potato

pretzel

pumpkin

puppet

purse

More to Do!

Little  went on a picnic. You can create a great picnic snack with help from an adult.

Perfect Picnic Mix

Ingredients:

(If there is something on the list you do not like, add something different to make your very own picnic mix.)

- 2 cups of small pretzels
- 2 cups of popped popcorn
- 1 cup of roasted, shelled peanuts
- 1 cup of dried peaches, cut into small pieces
- 2 cups of your favorite dry cereal
- 2 tablespoons of melted butter
- 1 teaspoon of cinnamon

Directions:

1. Mix the pretzels, popcorn, peanuts, peaches, and cereal in a large microwavable bowl.
2. Carefully drizzle the melted butter over the mixture.
3. Sprinkle with the cinnamon.
4. Gently stir everything together.
5. Place the bowl in the microwave and cook the mixture for 2 minutes.
6. Stir once more and enjoy!

About the Author

Best-selling author Jane Belk Moncure (1926–2013) wrote more than 300 books throughout her teaching and writing career. After earning a master's degree in early childhood education from Columbia University, she became one of the pioneers in that field. In 1956, she helped form the Virginia Association for Early Childhood Education, which established the first statewide standards for teachers of young children.

Inspired by her work in the classroom, Mrs. Moncure's books became standards in primary education, and her name was recognized across the country. Her success was reflected not only in her books' popularity with parents, children, and educators, but also by numerous awards, including the 1984 C. S. Lewis Gold Medal Award.

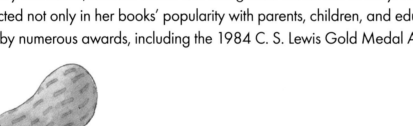

About the Illustrator

Rebecca Thornburgh lives in a pleasantly spooky old house in Philadelphia. If she's not at her drawing table, she's reading—or singing with her band, called Reckless Amateurs. Rebecca has one husband, two daughters, and two silly dogs.